The Princeton Diary

The Princeton Diary

Sparrow

Published by Vinal Publishing Inc.
193 Delaware Ave Buffalo NY 14202
Editor: Brett Axel
Cover art: Daniel Venekurt
ISBN: 978-1-7345036-0-9

The Princeton Diary

Milk frightens me – its wetness, its thickness, the way it's saturated with a meaningless color.

9

I have written four novellas, each with a one-word title: *Damp*, *Plus*, *Silver*, *Bale*. *Plus* was shortlisted for the McAllister Award.

Last night, I read in *The Princetonian*, was the best opportunity to see the aurora borealis in the last 10 years, so I dutifully walked outside at 1:23 AM. I saw no colors, just the mute mosque of the night sky.

Each time a rubber band breaks, I think, "I'll use this to make an artwork." But I never do.

I was reading *Phaedra* by Racine today. Here is one of the sleek lines I read:

> *Gardes, qu'Œnone sorte, et vienne seule ici.*

Princeton just had a Celebration of the Novel. I wasn't allowed on any of the panels – I'm not famous enough – but I went to all of the discussions and grew weary of the phrase "the arc of the novel." Why must every novel have an arc? Why not a zigzag, or a figure 8?

In my dream last night, I found a large-print edition of the *New Yorker* – the first I'd ever seen, awake or asleep. For hours I read an article by Michael Moore about jazz – unimaginative but addicting.

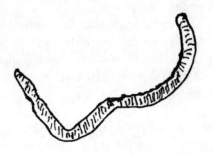

The early worm gets eaten.

More than any other creature (besides us) birds seem to be gossiping.

Floods are the result of temperature. In the winter, precipitation can continue for days with no problem; the water simply accumulates into higher and higher mounds. There are no floods in Antarctica. It's only when water liquefies that it's deadly.

Warhol discovered that, for our era, mock genius is more successful than real genius.

Today was a big fire in an apartment building near the university. I happened to be nearby – the cops cordoned off an area 500 feet around the fire. I stood on the periphery, as water from the fire hoses rose into the sky, sending up heroic columns of white steam. I almost told the cops, "I'm a fiction writer; I must get closer to take notes!" – but I lost my nerve.

How would one use a fire in a novella? Would the main character be burned out of his apartment? Or would a fire rage in the distance, a threat from the periphery? (Maybe even on TV?)

I've been depressed now for four days – a mild depression, almost a *literary* depression. For me sadness manifests as impatience. Everything in life goes too slowly. I step out of the shower and start dressing, but it takes three days to get my clothes on.

Last night a woman in a dream told me: "A fart is the grace of God." Even in the dream, I was struck by the oddness of this phrase. "I must remember that," I thought, and when I awoke, I did.

Today in the faculty lounge the coffee was gruesome
- far worse than ever before. "Do you know who made the coffee?" I asked several people, in a neutral tone, but no one would confess. I wasn't outraged so much as curious. How can one destroy coffee so thoroughly?

People who love living alone are people who love to fart.

My name is constantly being mispronounced – my last name, that is. Most people don't even realize it's Lithuanian; they think I'm Greek. The name is Kalavakas. It's a difficult word for Americans, though it contains only one vowel, always with the same intonation. (Its actual meaning is "small hill.")

America's two greatest poets: a queer man and a hermit woman (also contemporaries!).

Sparrow

I lost the extra key to my apartment, so I went to the locksmith to have it replaced. The key-maker was an alcoholic-looking Irishman of about 55. "We're starting to get a lot of business," he said, grinding my key.

"This season is big for losing keys?" I wondered. "Yeah, people are out more."

"What about in the winter? No one loses a key in the winter?"

"Joggers," he pronounced. "The keys fall out of their pockets onto the snow, and don't make a sound."

At a faculty party I met a young adjunct named Julia. She was radiant and blonde, with voluminous eyes. Using some pretext, I asked for her business card. It's the sharpest card I ever received: thick card stock cut with a Japanese knife. Presently it's digging into my thigh.

I allow myself the luxury of yawning. Sometimes at my favorite café, The Yellow Candle, I receive dirty looks from other habitués for over-yawning.

Today I stood in a field, watching a crow on the low branch of a budding tree. She called twice, then flew off. As she flew, I walked away – in imitation of her.

Here in Princeton if you dislike someone, you buy her an ugly gift or a shirt that doesn't fit. This is known as "grudge-shopping."

Last night I dreamed I was in London, walking. I came upon a new baseball stadium, just as the game was starting. I tried to find someone with an extra ticket, but no luck. Then I looked up and saw a home run fly out of the stadium… into the Thames!

I love a movie with a Beatnik Fight Scene.

The difference between Buddhism and Christianity: Buddha crucified himself.

When I was a child, my mother subscribed to the Sunset House Catalog, a delightful collection of devices, mostly for household use, all too eccentric to be sold at Sears. For some reason I vividly remember the illustration for a single sheet of opaque plastic covering an automobile. (Everything was illustrated with drawings; this was before the epidemic of photography.) My mother bought a gadget enabling her to place a telephone on her shoulder, freeing up her hands to do dishes, and other useful tasks. But when she actually used the harness, it was cumbersome and painful, and soon ended up in a cupboard above the stove.

What I always wanted from Sunset House was a large brown seed containing 100 tiny carved ivory elephants. Though it was only two dollars, my parents decreed it too frivolous. I would buy it now if I could find it.

"Sunset House" is an odd name for a mail-order company – the opposite of The House of the Rising Sun. One might write a song:

There is a house in Los Angeles They call the Setting Sun;
It's been the ruin of many catalog-readers, And Lord, I know I'm one.

From the first page, a novella-writer warns the reader: "Don't grow too cozy with these characters. In 80 pages they will die or move away. Keep your distance!"

Rain at night is like double night.

I rarely meet other novella-writers. One problem is economic. There's no market for novellas, unless they involve sex with dinosaurs.

Monotheism is a kind of atheism. The Hebrews disbelieved in thousands of gods. Thus, there remained only one – the number closest to zero.

I screwed up my courage to type "Sunset House" into Google Search. The company no longer exists, but I found a blog containing the "Best of Sunset House '64." The catalog was even stranger than I remembered! I had forgotten the "Nudie Ice Cubes": a "specially designed ice cube tray" which produced an endless supply of naked women, or rather naked "busts" of women (only from the waist up), smiling and posing with their hands behind their head (four different templates). The price: $1!

How characteristic of me to forget the naked ice- women while vividly recalling tiny elephants.

My friend Max Weberan is an artist. I bought a small oil painting from him, just 12" x 14", of a stream in the Poconos. It has a postimpressionist style, with lovely purplish shadows. I put it on the door of my bedroom, just to see how a painting looks hanging on a door. (Not bad!)

Princeton sits like a pampered cat on route 43. Knowing that I have precisely 3 years to live here, and will never dwell here again, makes me enjoy the place, as if I were on vacation in Venice.

Sometimes I walk into a house and think, "There's a piano somewhere." I sense a certain *authority* in the rooms that can only emerge from ivory keys.

A novel's a ship; a novella is a small sailboat. Novelists have flexibility; we can pivot.

Today I wet my hands just to spray droplets around the room.

My biggest literary influence is Polaroid. In the Princeton Library, I page through books of Polaroid photographs, admiring their wit and sexiness. "How can I produce the same effect in fiction?" I muse.

Most Americans tell time by their mortgages. ("That was in the third year of my second mortgage.")

Roughly once a month I have lunch with Joyce Carol Oates.

I do a great deal of walking, mostly around Princeton. When you walk, you notice trash on the ground. Often, I pick up an empty wrapper and carry it to the next garbage can.

UFOs, yetis and elves avoid photographers

How tragic that a guy can buy a skim milk latte at Starbucks, then throw the cup on the sidewalk and besmirch the name of his own coffeeshop!

I say "a guy" because I assume most garbage- throwers are male. I wonder what percentage of litter is created by men. At least 60%, I would say, but perhaps as much as 92%.

I don't miss my ex-wife, except at night. I loved the way she nestled in the sheets.

Car horns serve the same purpose as birdsong – to warn away rivals, or to express annoyance.

The Princeton postmistress always looks like she's about to dissolve into tears.

I wish I had a valet: someone to stand at attention behind me as I dressed, with an air of sympathetic obedience. (By the way, can a valet be female?)

According to the *Merriam-Webster Dictionary*, a valet must be male. (Synonym: "flunky")

I have night blindness. Normally, staring into blackness, I see nothing: no outlines, just vertiginous spreading voids.

Last night I dreamed I was at a Frank Zappa concert. At the end of the first set, Zappa began to play a solo, on a fancy electric cello he was holding. (Next to him was an elaborate rack from which the bows hung.) Zappa lifted his bow, drew it across a string, and… I just heard a grating sound. Why? Because the music required special headphones – big white 1960s-style headphones. Everyone else in the hall wore them. Where to get them? This anxiety awoke me.

The modern world isn't Shakespearean; it's Dantean.

I smoke about two cigarettes a year, usually in the winter. I like that ashen taste while walking on snow.

Every day I pay myself to sit and write. It's purely a ceremonial payment, but it gives me the encouraging sense that I have a "job." I get three dollars an hour, and I sit two hours – so when my writing is done, I have $6 to spend any way I like.

Sometimes I spend the money instantly, other times I hold on to it. Today I spent two days' "pay" on work gloves. I don't do any appreciable physical labor, but I like the feel of the thick cloth on my skin. Wearing these gloves, I feel stronger, almost brutish.

In a sense, we vote for celebrities. If millions of fans didn't see Tom Cruise movies, he'd soon disappear from *InStyle* magazine. We vote with our wallets.

I have a metaphysical nostalgia for the 3rd century CE. The radio is constantly begging me to buy gold - and I think I will! I want that particular metallic gleam in my apartment

Cigarettes are a stressful way of relieving stress.

Today, while walking on a deserted street, I came upon a disturbing sight: a woman's shoe, next to a white set of earbuds. Was someone raped there? Did a woman gaily throw off her footwear? Did a teenager toss his mother's shoe out the window of a Buick? And what about the earbuds? I can't invent a convincing scenario for them.

Once while I was traveling in Brazil, I drank red water. The woman I stayed with, a novelist, told me the water was red from mineral deposits. I stayed with her three days, and the whole time felt like I was drinking blood.

I have a binary mind: I'm either awake or asleep. I don't have forty successive veils of drowsiness, like most people. I lie in bed at night, collapse into a void of slumber, then jerk awake six hours later with no alarm.

Last night I dreamed ants were nesting in my hair. I extracted three of them – plus one incongruous dead fly – but there were more, I knew.

I love Princeton. When I first came here, I was slightly appalled; it's a little corner of New Jersey that aspires to be Connecticut. It seemed stiff, self- conscious – and it still feels that way. But now I admire its careful artificiality, the vain ambition that drives the place. Princeton is like a Victorian dollhouse. It's quaint despite its compulsion to be quaint.

Today I spent my six bucks on a taco and a Sprite.

Why does Joyce Carol Oates bother with me? She doesn't seem to like me particularly. (I don't blame her; I'm not especially appealing.) Perhaps she has a ritual of befriending, in a distant way, the person who holds my position. Or perhaps she pities me.

Soda cans are growing softer.

Coins are designed for the illiterate. A penny looks nothing like a dime; a quarter is obviously worth more than a nickel (because it's larger). Abraham Lincoln is not George Washington. Knowing no words, or even numbers, one can easily master all circular currency.

You know how when you talk to someone, you can obsessively fix your eyes on one feature? When I talk to Joyce Carol Oates, I constantly stare at her eyebrows.

I feel that I should give you my complete medical overview. I have arthritis in my left knee, a tendency towards very slight ear infections. If I climb a flight of stairs, I grow short of breath. My hair is thinning. Other than that, I am in fine health for 58.

I just discovered that caraway improves a salad dressing. Here's my recipe:

Ptarmigan's New Dressing

> 3 tablespoons virgin olive oil
> 1 tablespoon balsamic vinegar
> 1/16 teaspoon black pepper
> 1/16 teaspoon caraway seeds

(The title is meaningless, just a word I've always admired.)

Sparrow

Maybe I'm a narcissist, but when I walk in the rain I hear applause.

Oranges are becoming more ovular, less spherical, over the years. It's one of the small ways that humanity is improving.

I'm thinking to call my next book *Saliva*.

I was surprised how political Joyce Carol is. Her default conversational strategy is to complain about politics. Especially the politics of Texas, a place she despises.

Before living here, I was in Boulder, so this is a nice transition to the east. If I had moved directly into Philadelphia, I might have had a nervous breakdown.

Today I spent my six dollars on mushrooms. I stuffed them with a combination of thyme (from a plant growing in my kitchen), chopped pine nuts and rice. I roasted them, then served them to myself. They were magnificent.

Songbirds try to wake us every morning, but we have invented soundproof windows.

My ex-wife, Anne, called me – called me, rather than emailed – to ask for a meeting. She didn't explain why. Next Tuesday we'll dine in a neutral restaurant in New Brunswick.

One of nature's puns: anthills and volcanoes. They are strangely similar in structure, though not in size. Why? Because lava pours out of one, ants out of the other.

Anne always calls, rather than emails. She doesn't want our non-relationship to become *formal*.

Today, while walking, I noticed that the shadow of a moth is lovelier than a moth.

My novella is going very badly. It's set in the Deep South during the Civil War, in a town called Globeville. I'm trying to write a story of the whole town, a little like *Winesburg, Ohio*. It's a very ambitious book, but I have written ambitious books before that have succeeded. *The New York Times Book Review* called my last novella "a Matterhorn of prose." This one fails and fails again. Every day, at the end of the three hours, the page wins, and I lose. I would tear up the whole book, but I can't – it's inside my computer. I'd have to print it out first, which is ridiculous. "Deleting" the manuscript is not enough. I want to rip it up, physically, with my hands.

Maybe there's another book I'm *meant* to be writing – but what? A history of the Danish Parliament? A comparative study of geodes? I must speak to a psychic.

I don't love money;
I let money love me.

I met with Anne, in a too-cute restaurant called Arthur's. I had French toast; she had a fruit salad. Her concern is three boxes of books that are still in her storage unit. I went through a period of obsession with James Fenimore Cooper, so I have a number of his works, plus scholarly studies of him. I was going to write a novella set in Western Pennsylvania in the 18th century – one of my many ideas that later fizzled.

I promised to pick up the books, though typically, we didn't set a date. My ex-wife looked happy, though wary. I suspect she just wanted to see me, and confirm that she was "winning."

Is she in love? Of course she didn't say.

It's remarkable that I can talk to Anne for an hour and learn nothing about her life. It's like meeting a spy. All I get is her "cover story."

I have joined the atheists club, which is actually called Atheists of Princeton. My thinking was, "I don't go to church, but I want to meet people." So far I've been to two meetings. A woman named Elizabeth fascinates me. She's very pretty, but also looks a bit like an ape. All through the meeting I watched her, usually out of the corner of my eye (but not always, because she is a very active member of this group.) Her face is constantly changing, in response to the conversation.

I have always liked the name Elizabeth – and despised the name Liz. "Liz" never has the happy breeziness of "Betty" or "Sue" – or even "Peg." If you must shorten Elizabeth, why not the sonorous old name "Eliza"?

If Adam had never asked for a "helpmeet" he'd probably still be in Eden: healthy, peaceful, slightly lonely.

God is right-wing; the angels are Socialist.

My novella continues to go nowhere. It's like trying to light a book of matches that's fallen in the toilet. Maybe my problem is the title – or rather the lack of a title. A great book should flow effortlessly from its title. I've never really had a name for this manuscript.

Here, let me open the dictionary at random: pooh-pooh

Not a bad title for a novella! (*The American Heritage Dictionary of the English Language* gives this definition: "To express contempt for or impatience about; make light of." Next comes this example: "*British actors have long pooh-poohed the Method*" (Stephen Schiff). Then they helpfully explain that the word originates as a "reduplication of POOH.")

I heard one of my colleagues call an elaborate brunch a "bruncheon."

Today I could hear a voice from the next apartment saying: "I have an idea!" The speaker was female and sounded fairly young – in her 20s. I heard two other voices immediately expressing interest, but I couldn't hear exactly what they said. And I couldn't make out what the idea was. People say, "I have an idea!" much louder than they explain the idea.

I feel that I am falling in love with someone, but I don't know who. Someone far away, I believe. (Maybe a man?) Will I ever meet this lover?

I asked Joyce Carol Oates: "Is it possible to love someone you've never met; someone you know nothing about?"

"Absolutely," she answered. "I am in love with six or seven people I don't know. That's why I write. My books are for them."

Sparrow

"Do you want to meet them?"

"Oh, no. It's not that sort of love. It's a blind love, a love without details. That's what the books are; they fill in the details."

Today I walked close enough to a robin to see its glittering, cold eye.

Every morning I sit at my desk, attempting to write. Two hours goes quite slowly when you're not writing. I refuse to read or amuse myself in any way. Actually, not writing is much more difficult than writing.

I stood in line at the fruit stand, next to two young parents and two young children. The woman pushed a disconsolate boy in a stroller; the man held a toddler by the hand. The wife had brown glasses, a librarian face, and two round, bold, declarative breasts. (It was a warm spring day, and she wore only a t-shirt.) The man was clearly a Muslim – a curling beard *sans* mustache, a brownish face. The two of them spoke for a while, before he handed off the boy; he was heading to school, either as student or professor. (I know because the woman said: "Have a good class!") What was most striking was how the woman smiled confidingly, leaning towards him. She was flirting with her own husband! I stood, with an avocado and two tomatoes, awed by the presence of love.

I spend a lot of my time thinking of witty remarks for Joyce Carol Oates. Much of this journal is a rehearsal for our lunches.

The last time I saw Joyce she was wearing a kimono with a paisley design. Attached to the kimono was a cape. It was the weirdest outfit I've ever seen on a lunch companion. I was almost paralyzed with mystification. Of course, there was no way to diplomatically ask about her attire.

Princeton has the inertness of a ceramic castle in a fishbowl.

Little-known fact: Joyce Carol Oates' closest friends call her "JC," as if to suggest the parallels between her and Jesus.

Joyce herself never mentions this.

I left my umbrella by the front door of my apartment, and forgot to bring it in. This morning it was gone – stolen either by a man or by the wind.

There's very little theft in Princeton. Probably the wind was the culprit.

Sparrow

I went to the Dollar General store, in Clydesdale. (There isn't one in Princeton.) My goal was to spend my daily six dollars. I overheard a black guy saying: "My wife got custody of the kids, then her mother sued her for custody, then the mother got custody, then I sued *her* for custody. Because my mother-in- law was unfit — it was obvious!" But then he walked away, and I never found out if he received custody. (I bought raisins and a tiny flashlight.)

When you press the button on an elevator, you can feel it thinking: a meager, but palpable thought.

Any species of bird might be a verb. One could speak of someone "seagulling," or "nightingaling" or "eagling." I wonder why our language doesn't have more of such words. (There are thousands of birds, but only three bird-verbs: "parroting," "hawking" and "crowing.")

As a child, if I cut myself, my mother would produce a small bottle of iodine tincture and paint my wound. The bottle was brown; the top had a plastic wand attached to it. The iodine itself was a distinctive brown purple. Does anyone still do this?

It was the intersection of visual art and Victorian medicine.

"God" is probably a metaphor for the sun. All earthly life emerges from the power of one celestial being, in truth.

No great poet ever used mouthwash.

Even if "God" doesn't exist, we see our "god" above us daily.

All novelists feel inferior to poets. I've begun to memorize poems to recite to JC. I started with this one by Tennyson:

Lilian

I

Airy, Fairy Lilian, Flitting, fairy Lilian,
When I ask her if she love me, Claps her tiny hands above
me, Laughing all she can;
She 'll not tell me if she love me, Cruel little Lilian.

II

When my passion seeks Pleasance in love-sighs,
She, looking thro' and thro' me
Thoroughly to undo me,
Smiling, never speaks:
So innocent-arch, so cunning-simple,
From beneath her gathered wimple
Glancing with black-bearded eyes,
Till the lightning laughters dimple
The baby-roses in her cheeks;
Then away she flies.

III

Prythee weep, May Lilian!
Gaiety without eclipse
Wearieth me, May Lilian;
Thro' my every heart it thrilleth
When from crimson-threaded lips
Silver-treble laughter trilleth:
Prythee weep, May Lilian!

IV

Praying all I can,
If prayers will not hush thee,
Airy Lilian,
Like a rose-leaf I will crush thee,
Fairy Lilian.

That's a pretty weird poem!

Sparrow

Though Joyce Carol is modest, she has an air of greatness. Dining with her is like conferring with Winston Churchill, or Archimedes.

I found a pair of eyeglasses on a table at Starbucks. I didn't notice them until I sat down. Just as an experiment, I tried on the spectacles. The lenses were strong: they stretched out the room and twisted it. I stood up and walked towards the bathroom, feeling like I was on mescaline. Then I took off the glasses and read the *Times*.

I'm one of the few professors who doesn't wear glasses. When I'm around the faculty, my eyes feel conspicuously naked.

I went on a "cow adventure," driving around looking at cows. I wonder if Joyce Carol likes cows? I will describe it to her the next time I see her.

Every three days, without fail, I masturbate – always in my bed, late at night. (Usually a little after 12.)

The wind kills very few animals, but routinely murders trees.

"I've only been an intellectual two weeks!"

The Old Testament prophets were extremely damaged individuals – creepy misanthropes who got their kicks predicting the destruction of Israel (and occasionally other empires). Their language is often exalted, but it's easy to write that way when you're angry and unhinged.

I have hay fever, which manifests as sinus headaches. Today I feel like a towel is balled up between my brain and my right eyebrow.

Sparrow

People with cats spend much of their time trying to keep their pets from escaping. They're like antebellum slaveowners.

I can feel my wife pumping resentment into the atmosphere, 220 miles away.

Princeton is what New Jersey would be like without the Mafia.

Henry James, William James, Frank James, and Jesse James were all contemporaries.

At our near-monthly luncheon today, Joyce Carol stared right through her omelet.

"I went on a cow adventure," I told her. "Where did you go?" she asked.

"Up by Point Margrave."

"And what exactly was your cow adventure?" she asked, somewhat ironically.

"I drove past cows. Twice I got out and looked at them. One cow was close enough to speak to."

"What did you say to her?" "I told her my problems."

"And what did she say?"

"Nothing. She was listening, but she didn't even moo."

"She's a Freudian," Joyce decreed, with a slight smile.

But she didn't ask what my problems were.

Also, she really loved the Tennyson poem.

Everyone assumes that religion is well-intended, because it speaks about love and patience and gentleness. But so do evil sociopaths! Serial killers, when they meet you on the street, say: "You must learn to trust people more."

The dawn today was singular: radiating ecstasies of orange, lavender and pink through the sky.

Joyce Carol never discusses her writing, or her novels. Talking to her, you might think she was an accountant or a brickmason. What's surprising is how often she mentions her childhood in upstate New York. "My father once got cheated by a horse trader," she told me yesterday. "The trader was an Armenian, who filed down the teeth of a gelding to make the horse look younger. Once my father discovered the trick, he was furious!" Joyce smiled.

Joyce's father was, for many years, a farmer.

Hair is unaffected by gravity. The rest of my body is always pulled down; my hair spurts upwards.

Sparrow

I found this entry in an old journal:

Alaska and Hawaii

Alaska and Hawaii entered the United States in 1959.

Together they include 1,402 islands.

I want to write a more realistic story – maybe one about a woman who works in a laundromat. But I can't *imagine* a woman who works in a laundromat. This is where I'm stuck.

The sky today is withdrawn, noncommittal – almost no color.

I had the urge to throw a rock, so I drove to a stream outside of town. I found a small rounded stone and tossed it into the water, where it disappeared swiftly. It's spring, time to throw rocks!

Something awful is happening to my upper back. It's like the bones are disappearing – as if my inherent spinelessness is becoming literal

Movies are illusions;
popcorn is real.

Sparrow

Princeton University kindly supplies me with a writing room. They call it my "office," but it's small and severe, with metal shelves. I have left it unadorned, except for a photograph of Dostoevsky. In it Fyodor looks young, his beard wispy. His arms are crossed; he wears a wide-lapel coat with two large symmetrical buttons. Dostoevsky stares intently off to the side, as if puzzled by some interior question. All in all, the Russian prophet looks rather like a minor Civil War general – which he might have been, had he been born in our nation.

The purpose of this photo is not "inspiration." Its purpose is closer to "discouragement." I suspect that if I threw away Fyodor's image, I might start writing again, but I am stubborn. I want Dostoevsky watching over me, which he literally does. His eyes are focused just above my right shoulder.

When leaves first appear in springtime, they are totally different than they will be – so delicate and pastel-green. It's like trees full of salad.

You know how takeout Chinese restaurants always have a little shrine to Buddha? Usually there's one or two fresh oranges on it, and a stick of incense. You never see the workers worshiping at the shrine, but they always have one. I always want to ask about these altars, but I can't think of a question.

I heard "Your Song" by Elton John in the supermarket. I was struck how skillfully Elton John, then completely closeted, solved the problem of writing a gay love song for Top 40 radio. The answer was to use the second person:

> It's a little bit funny, this feeling inside;
> I'm not one of those who can easily hide.
> I don't have much money but, boy, if I did,
> I'd buy a big house where we both could live.

"A little bit funny," "easily hide," "boy": these were clues that none of us noticed (except, perhaps, other gay people?).

When I tell a lie, I am always caught. It's uncanny. That's why I started writing fiction: it's the only safe place I can dispense untruths.

When I read the world's scriptures, I'm ashamed for the human race. The gods we've created are a bunch of willful, defiant babies – pretending to be Fathers.

Last night my clock radio suddenly went mad. The numbers began spinning around for no reason, making a strangulated sound as if the clock were possessed by a demon. I quickly unplugged it.

Today the clock is still dark, of course.

I find Joyce Carol's novels turgid and repetitive; I've never made it all the way through one. (One reason I write novellas is that most novels strike me as far too long.) For me, her greatest work of art is herself: this birdlike 74-year-old with a child's eyes, perched on the edge of a chair, looking alternately like a princess and a servant.

As soon as I wake up, I make my bed. I consider making the bed an art – perhaps not a *high* art, but certainly an art, like ceramics.

Am I the only person who's ever tried to write the Great American Novella?

I met Joyce Carol again, for lunch, and this time she wore a simple purple sweater and blue pants. (Not jeans, blue pants.) Her outfit was as minimal as the previous one was bizarre. Was she making a *statement*?

Today during my writing time, I produced 16 pages, which I promptly tore up. It's my largest output so far: a complete short story, called "The Apple Splits," about a young woman named Heliodora living in London in 1917 – influenced by a biography of H. D. I've been reading. The story was awful, but had a few good lines, such as: "She asked for crisps, but immediately reconsidered."

I am like Penelope, who tears apart each night her day's weaving.

What does "putter" literally mean? Nowadays it's used only in one sense – "I'm puttering around the house" – but I can't imagine the ancient English invented a word to mean "walking idly around, occasionally folding a scarf or writing a check." How many people puttered around in the year 832? Probably only kings and dukes.

According to my dictionary, "putter" is "probably frequentative of middle English *poten*, to poke, push." Which explains why a golf club that gently pushes the ball is called a putter. ("I'm just poking around my apartment" would be a literal meaning.) A "frequentative," as you may have guessed, expresses repeated action. ("I'm just poking and poking around my apartment" would be a more precise translation.)

Only two species get panic attacks: cats and humans.

I want to brew my own beer. I'll probably start with a porter, which is the easiest to brew, I've heard. I've already started thinking of names for my "brand." My favorite so far: "Bewilderment Beer."

Crows are so loud they sound like they're using microphones.

I asked Joyce Carol about writer's block; does it ever happen to her? "Of course," she said. "Everyone has writer's block! I've been trying to write a historical novel about Montaigne for the last 35 years. It's impossible; I'm stuck. All my other books are feeble attempts to fill that void."

When I was a youth, all televisions were three-dimensional; they were essentially cubes. Now they're almost as thin as cardboard.

Originally, I wanted to be a bookbinder, before I began seriously writing. If my writer's block continues, I hope to pursue that profession. I've always wanted to make books; my mistake was thinking that I should personally write them.

One of Joyce Carol's arms is noticeably longer than the other. (Her right is longer than her left – and she's left-handed!)

I was buying contact lens solution at CVS today, and I noticed the name tag of the clerk: Jalissa. She was a pretty woman of about 21, who looked Dominican. "Are you the only Jalissa on earth?" I asked her.

She smiled. "I've never met another," she admitted.

"Did your mother invent your name?"

"She was going to call me Alissa, but her sister said to her, 'Why not Jalissa?'"

"Do you like your name?" "I guess so."

"It sounds Muslim."

"No one ever said that to me."

She was getting embarrassed, so I ended my conversation. When someone works in retail, their name is public – their first name, that is.

Rain slows a day. The sound it produces on a rooftop – *tidda-tidda-tippida-tidda-tippida* – has a narcotic effect on the mind.

Though she's not Jewish, and isn't married to a Jew, Joyce Carol often says, "Mazel tov," to mean "congratulations," for any achievement. She pronounces it very Jewishly, and the whole experience is a bit mystifying.

Walking in the woods, I thought I saw a soft pretzel - but it was a brown curling leaf. This was the first pretzel-mirage I've seen.

At Atheists of Princeton, a woman named Pam Mathiesen lectured on "Religion and War." Before the spread of nationalism in the late 18th century – and even afterwards – the best reason for sustained human slaughter has always been God.

I brush my teeth diagonally. I've been doing it for years.

Everyone, as a child, tries praying for what they want, and it doesn't work. That's why no one believes in God. (Yes, people *say* they believe in God, but what do they mean by that? They know they're supposed to believe, and they feel some faint gratitude for being alive, but they never think about the Deity. How can you think about Him? It's like thinking about pure yellow. God is an abstraction.)

No one says to herself, "I hope I die soon, so I may go to Heaven and be with God." I mean, no one over the age of seven.

How long must you live in a place until you have a right to describe its climate? A year? Eight months? ("I spent eight months in Timor; it has a lovely climate.")

I found a pleasing wine: Badger Mountain Riesling (2006). It's light, organic, from Vermont. It tastes like the kiss of a 23 year old girl.

My ex-wife was allergic to me – not literally, but metaphorically. At first, she mistook this allergy for attraction. But after living together for six weeks, everything I did appalled her. She liked me personally, but was helpless before her revulsion. Eventually she asked me to leave, for her own health. Of course, I agreed.

I don't believe in genius. Even Shakespeare had to write play after play, year after year, until he stumbled upon brilliance. If Shakespeare was a true genius, how could he have written *The Life and Death of King John*?

I've begun to picture Joyce Carol Oates while I'm masturbating. I don't see myself having sex with her; rather I picture her in a white shroud standing above me. As I moan, she looks down, frowning.

Everything on earth has a longitude and latitude – even a glass of milk.

I get carsick, seasick, and horsesick. (That is, I become nauseous while riding on a horse.) But air travel doesn't disturb me. Taking an airplane is not like traveling. It's more like sitting still while the world revolves beneath you.

In the 19th century, if an audience wildly applauded the movement of a symphony, the conductor would play it again. Has anyone tried that in literature? After the best chapter of your novel, leave a blank page, then repeat it.

Today I heard a bird say:

speh speh speh speh speh speh speh speh speh
speh speh speh speh speh speh speh speh speh
speh speh speh speh speh speh speh speh speh
speh speh speh speh speh speh speh speh speh
speh speh speh speh speh speh speh speh speh
speh speh speh speh speh speh speh speh speh
speh speh speh speh speh speh speh speh speh
speh speh speh speh speh speh speh speh speh

Does Bob Dylan ever get a Bob Dylan song stuck in his head?

Last night I dreamed that the stores in Princeton were closing – not for the evening, but forever. As I walked down the streets, one store after another was empty: a flower shop, a deli, a bookstore. It was a Princeton Apocalypse.

I've always loved the phrase "door prize."

Most of us forget – if we ever knew – that the sky is divided into "lanes," for airplanes to ride through, like trucks on a highway. The firmament has been mapped as precisely as Arizona.

The last time I spoke to Joyce CO, she said, "We don't need the Ku Klux Klan anymore – we have the police!" She makes these "radical" remarks sometimes – to provoke me? I'm not sure. One can tell nothing from her face.

I made a successful Greek salad: red romaine lettuce, grape tomatoes, Greek olives, feta cheese, golden raisins. A triumph! (My secret: a tiny pinch of cinnamon.)

Religious people are fond of saying, "You must have faith in *something*," but that's untrue. You can enter an abandoned house and proceed tentatively across the floor, fearful that it may collapse. You can walk without trust; in fact, it's wiser to do so. Doubt may be your guide, as much as faith.

Pillows have faces. You can definitely see mouths and eyes – even nostrils. It's quite possible, by manipulating a pillow, to give it a human expression. You can teach a pillow to smile.

The Atheists Club assigned *The Future of an Illusion* by Sigmund Freud. It was his anti-God manifesto; I'm halfway through. The book is precisely written and makes a compelling psychological point: we all experienced a Huge Father in the Sky when we were children. Our powerful father hovered above us, predicting our needs. Even as three-year-olds, we correctly intuit that this enormous being has brought us into existence. Years later, we recognize that our dad is just a human being, but we prolong our childish security through a belief in God. Religion, in short, is nostalgia for infancy.

Photography is mostly luck, but a great photographer *attracts* luck.

After my wife threw me out, the first thing I did was buy a telescope. Each night I'd look up at the stars – even if it was cloudy and I only saw two or three. For some reason, I found the universe soothing.

There's a small Cy Twombly show at the Princeton Museum: several of his late, drippy paintings, and eight sculptures. The sculptures look like toolboxes next to a cabin in Idaho.

I love the name "Cy Twombly." It would be a good title for a novella (and in that book I'd never mention the artist!)

What are Joyce Carol's tastes in art? I've never asked her. One can imagine her loving Whistler – or alternately being oblivious to every painting.

I looked it up; Cy Twombly's real name is Edwin Parker.

I'm the only person I know who eats breadcrumbs and cookie crumbs mixed together, as a dessert.

Yesterday I had lunch with Joyce Carol. Fifteen minutes into our conversation, I thought I saw her twitch. *Is she getting old?* I wondered. *Does she have a palsy?*

Then immediately, I was ashamed.

Sherlock Holmes is much smarter than me-

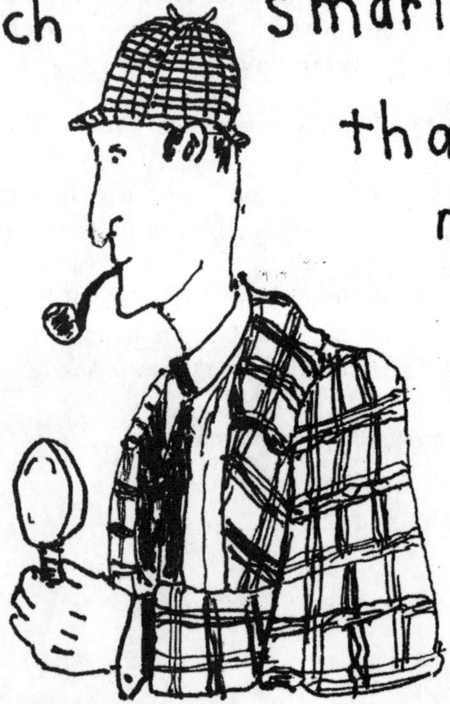

but he doesn't exist!

My masturbation fantasy with Joyce continues, except that now at the climactic moment, she unsheathes a sword.

After our luncheons, I re-examine the conversation for hints about her own sex life – but I've found none. She never mentions beds, romantic vacations, any traces of bodily intimacy.

All religions demean women. Why? Because they posit a mythical male Creator, whereas in reality each of us is born from a woman.

It's difficult to write gravity into a novel. Most novelists describe a world that's weightless.

My sex with Anne was always high-powered. When I would enter her, it felt like sirens were going off all over North America. The sensation wasn't exactly pleasurable; it was *momentous*. (But did she feel the same way? I never asked.)

Music is best
understood
as "invisible
painting."

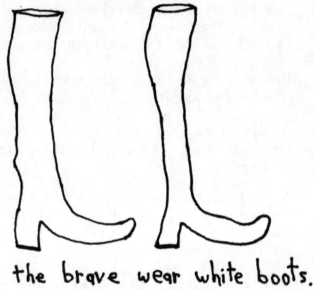

Only the brave wear white boots.

It's fascinating to watch Joyce Carol eat. She glares at the food as if it were an ancient enemy, then patiently slices a sliver of squash and deposits it in her mouth.

A big wind blew today – a boastful wind.

I sit at my desk every day, unfailingly, for two hours – sometimes a little longer. In front of me are two sharpened No. 2 pencils and a yellow legal pad. Usually I write nothing, but every few days I commit some words to paper, either in a great stream or painfully, one by one. Afterwards, I reread what I've written and find it worthless. Then I throw it away (or rather recycle it). I haven't written a word that I've saved for eight months.

Usually I tear up my daily writings. I find it very pleasurable to rip up the pages, one by one.

A neighbor left an orange plastic ball in the courtyard. Now it's gleaming in the morning sun, like a too-round pumpkin.

Has Joyce Carol written more books than any other living writer? I doubt it. More than any other living woman? Unlikely. Her achievement is writing the greatest number of "literary" books.

What about Stephen King? Who has more – him or her?

I just looked Joyce Carol up on the Internet. The University of San Francisco, for some reason, has the complete list of her books. I counted 51 novels, 12 novellas, 6 young adult books, 38 collections of short stories, 8 collections of poetry, 3 children's books, 14 volumes of nonfiction, 9 books of plays. (But I won't include the 22 anthologies she's edited.) I get 135. That has to be more than Stephen King. (Maybe she *is* the world's most prolific living writer.) Four or five of those categories surprised me. Joyce Carol has more books of poems than most serious poets!

Thank God she's at Princeton. Without that imprimatur she might seem like a *hack*.

Does she collect all these books, physically, in a room somewhere? I've only been to her house once, for a stiff little dinner party, and the six of us were strictly herded into the dining room – the rest of the house was effectively cordoned off.

For Stephen King, all I could find was a list of his novels: 67. But I don't believe he has books of plays, poetry, biographies of American artists, etc. (Which reminds me, I was wondering about Joyce Carol's artistic tastes. She wrote a biography of George Bellows! Which connects to her nonfiction book, *On Boxing*!)

What is the secret of Joyce Carol's prolificacy? Does she take dictation from an Inner Voice? Does she borrow plots from Tolstoy? Is she compelled to write exactly 1700 lines a day

I sit at my writing desk producing nothing, while she cheerfully types out her 136th book. She will be remembered; I will be forgotten.

A bird outside my window is insistently singing, "Be, be, be, be, be" – over and over, in five-note phrases.

Now that I'm drug-free, everyone offers me free drugs.

Every daddy longlegs I've seen this spring has an orange body. Is this new? Or have I never noticed their color before?

I borrowed a Joyce Carol Oates novella from the Princeton Library: *Black Water*. Here's the first paragraph:

The rented Toyota, driven with such impatient exuberance by the Senator, was speeding along the unpaved unnamed road, taking the turns in giddy skidding slides, and then, with no warning, somehow the car had gone off the road and had overturned in black rushing water, listing to its passenger's side, rapidly sinking.

It sounds like she wrote it on the way to a dentist appointment!

Wine tastes better mixed with a little dust. Just pick up a bit of dust from your floor or bookshelf and sprinkle it in your glass of rosé. You'll notice the difference.

If I could have any superpower, what would it be? I can't decide. Maybe the power to turn into glycerin?

There's a woman next door to me – I think of her as The Lonely Woman with the Dog. I don't know her first name; on the doorbell downstairs is written "Wilson." She's maybe 32. I would call her a *belle laide* - an attractive woman who isn't conventionally pretty – but that phrase is no longer used. The Lonely Woman With the Dog barely nods to me; she's deeply involved with her noisy little dog. Suddenly, in the last three weeks, a handsome boyfriend has appeared; I've seen him two or three times. He's deferential, gentle. I'm so happy for her! I want to say, "It's so wonderful that you've found love" – but I am silent.

Joyce Carol's writing spills out of her, like conversation from an alcoholic. It feels uncontrolled, gushing. Yet her conversation is precise and measured.

I love doo-wop. For some reason, I haven't mentioned this yet. Lately I'm listening to The Jive Bombers.

When I think of my ideal reader, I always picture a nine-year-old girl with a ragged haircut and a crooked smile. I hope this doesn't mean I'm a pedophile.

I suspect that Joyce Carol is hypnotizing me into an obsession with her. She must have that power; how else can one publish 135 books? There's something pathetic about me running my finger along the computer screen, counting her volumes of nonfiction — but she has manipulated the whole world into such a fascination. That's what "fame" is: mass hypnosis.

Today I made a salad of spinach, fresh corn (cut from the cob), cooked beets, and a spicy paprika dressing.

I've considered writing a doo-wop novella, but how exactly to do it? I am utterly unqualified. In fact I may be unqualified to write anything. I have no life experience. I've never been a sniper, an adulterer, a mechanic, a detective. Aesop, who was a freed slave, could write amazing stories like:

The Lion in Love

A lion once fell in love with a beautiful maiden and proposed marriage to her parents. The old people did not know what to say. They didn't wish to give their daughter to the lion, yet they feared enraging the King of Beasts. At last the father replied: "We feel highly honored by Your Majesty's proposal, but, you see, our daughter is a tender youth, and we fear that in the vehemence of your affection you might possibly do her some injury. Might I venture to suggest that your Majesty should have your claws removed, and your teeth extracted? Then we would gladly consider your proposal again."

The lion was so much in love that he had his claws trimmed and his teeth pulled out. But when he came again to the parents, they simply laughed in his face and bade him do his worst.

Moral: Love can tame the wildest beast.

I'm a literary private detective, trying to solve the mystery of Joyce Carol Oates. One good source of knowledge is her tweets. Joyce Carol's Twitter account is like a vast haiku-autobiography – perhaps unique in world literature.

Even though poets no longer celebrate dew, it still appears every morning, alert and glittering

Sparrow

When you admire doo-wop, you learn to hide your passion. It strikes most people as an affectation, or worse, nostalgia. I have no yearning for the 1950s. Are fans of Erik Satie idealizing the 1890s?

I went to the Atheist meeting today. The people are very nice – almost scrupulously nice – but I get a little nervous I will inadvertently use the word "God" – as in "O my God!" – and alienate everyone. No doubt this is a neurotic fear. (Though no one else seems to say it.)

The ape-woman was present, but on the other side of the room, and we didn't speak.

When I was married, I belonged to the mass of heterosexuals. Going to the movies with my wife, I was part of the Majority. Now I'm like a gay man, an orphan, a transsexual – an outsider. I have joined the Numerous Minorities.

I saw the Lonely Woman With the Dog and the boyfriend, walking her pet. The dog is also falling in love with him!

Doo-wop was invented in echoing spaces: in stairwells, on subway platforms, under bridges. It is a musical tribute to the caverns of urban architecture.

I ate a nectarine so ripe it tasted like ice cream.

The Princeton Diary

A snake appeared in my apartment! I was sweeping the hall closet, and I noticed a small movement; at first I thought it was a loose electrical cord. Then I realized it was a serpent, with beige stripes.

A striped snake! Aren't they poisonous? What should I do? I ran to the kitchen, seized a plastic container, and attempted to capture the reptile – but she was too fast. However, I positioned the container, she'd wriggle away. Finally, I picked her up by the tail. She spun around to bite me, but I tossed her quickly out the door. Then I laughed, almost hysterically, to myself. "A reptilian visitor!" I said aloud.

People my age are called "The Soft Generation." Most of us have never done any physical labor – not even gardening.

In the last eight months, I've written the equivalent of an 800-page (postmodern) novel – then ripped it to shreds. Maybe I could teach a course in "creative non-writing."

A number of major doo-wop singers are still alive. For example, Jerome Gourdine, the "Little Anthony" of Little Anthony & The Imperials, is 78. He is one of our greatest living vocalists and is almost completely forgotten.

Sparrow

I never buy celery; it's too painful. I like the taste in soups, but my mother served me celery sticks throughout my youth, so I have a horror of this nutritious "snack."

How can I continue with this 'career'? How much longer can I teach writing when I myself do not write? Should I hire a ghostwriter for my next novella? I could give her – I would prefer a woman – the basic instructions: "Write about a doo-wop singer named Terry who lives in Baltimore, with his girlfriend Janine. She has two young children from a previous relationship. Terry is 43; his singing career is over. He works at a small record company, sweeping the floor and doing a little paperwork. Every day he sees 'successful' artists – singers and musicians – who pass him as if he's invisible. Terry's life continues until one day he decides… what? To go back to school? To kill someone? To revive his career?" I'll let the ghostwriter work out the details. Or is this whole plan morally wrong?

I stumbled upon a display of 18th and 19th century American maps in Princeton's geography department. (They have a small gallery.) Two of the maps had been eaten by bookworms. The little burrows they made through the paper suggest geographic features: a tunnel between Maryland and Virginia, for example.

The first doo-wop singers were poor; they couldn't afford instruments. No matter how broke you are, you still have a voice.

After my wife kicked me out, I cried for three days. Admittedly, it was only about two minutes a day, but I did cry daily. After that, my weeping ceased – except while watching *The Little Mermaid*.

I've had very little success with women, but on the other hand, I also haven't had much success with men.

Maybe I should give up on writing fiction and just perfect an essay on doo-wop…

I told Joyce Carol the snake-in-the-closet story. It was an enormous success, probably the most impressive anecdote I've recounted to her. She asked me to describe the creature three times. She didn't take notes, but I have the sickening feeling that my snake will soon appear in a Joyce Carol Oates short story.

Today I stood beneath a maple tree in the rain, listening to raindrops falling on the leaves. This is how I'd like to write, I thought – not with weary words, but with multitudinous pattering.

A new idea: I should write the snake short story, faster than Joyce Carol, and win at least one small victory.

Mormon missionaries are always two teenage guys in suits and ties, living together for two years. Do they ever fall in love?

Crows can make a sound that is simultaneously an "h" and a "k." One might write it as:

(Hk)a (hk)a a (hk)a

Hollyhocks and azaleas are blooming outside my apartment. They are so celebratory – like pantsuits from 1974!

I like Anne – perhaps I don't love her, but I like her. But I never enjoy seeing her, because it feels like I broke her arm and it will never heal.

Night falls hard in Princeton – and early. Princetonians take a positive pleasure in going to sleep.

I began my short story about the snake:

> Kate Hawthorne was a stewardess. She lived in Lexington, Kentucky. This was her 13th year with an airline; her first five were with Delta, the rest with Continental. Kate worked four days on, three days off – she had seniority. Like most flight attendants, she usually stayed home on her days

> off. After you've traveled to Madrid and back, it's nice to confine yourself to a four-block radius.

> I want to suggest a tie to Nathaniel Hawthorne; that's why I chose that name. And it seems logical

that a person who works in the sky would see a snake in her apartment. (But this is just a first draft – which I will probably discard.)

In my current Joyce Carol masturbation fantasy, she wears a mask and chatters like a bullfinch.

I find the absence of a God comforting. Without a stern Creator standing over me in judgment, I can freely live my small, elusive life.

Princeton is neither a town nor a city; officially, it's a "borough." It has 14,203 inhabitants. I'm constantly walking through it, and know it quite well, yet I'm almost certain that once I leave, at the end of my tenure here, I will never return.

By writing on paper then tearing it up, I am avoiding computers entirely. I could be living in 1903. (The ballpoint pen was invented in 1888.)

I can't imagine having facial hair. It strikes me as a burden, like wearing a bag of sand around your neck.

Christians often say: "Without God, what is the basis of morality?" – but that's absurd. All the moral laws were written by humans, not by a Supreme Being. The Deity was just a pretext, and may be dropped, like any pseudonym.

Sparrow

I hate the term "writer's block." For one thing, it's archaic. It feels like it belongs to the 1930s. For another, it's an inadvertent pun – as if one is speaking about an actual "block" – like a block of wood. I need to find another word. Maybe "speechlessness"?

The first doo-wop song was 1950. The first sex change operation was Christine Jorgensen in 1951. Both of these innovations question the boundaries of gender. The black musicians who invented doo- wop realized that recorded music is anonymous: you can't *see* the singers. Therefore, you can't know who's a man and who's a woman. And what does it mean to be a woman? Auditorily, it means to have a high voice. The sound of a high falsetto breaking free of the chanted backdrop is the sound of a male transforming into a female.

The sky today resembles an unappetizing bowl of oatmeal.

I'm a walker, not a bicyclist. (I'm tempted, actually, to call myself a "walkist.") I prefer to travel standing, not sitting.

Today I spent my six dollars on a bandanna, which I tied around my head. I look like an ineffectual Bruce Springsteen.

I've decided on the superpower that I want: to breathe in oxygen and breathe out viruses – fast- acting viruses that quickly kill any villain. (But what will be my superhero-name will? "ViroMan?")

I'm not a mountaineer; I'm a hilleer.

Why did I originally become a writer? I have a memory of my mother reading me *The Pokey Little Puppy* when I was four. At one point she mentioned that someone wrote this story. This astounded me. I had assumed that storybooks came from some eternal netherworld. I didn't know that a person like myself could write one. This planted the fatal seed in my mind that now leads me to sit at my desk every day, speechlessly, for two hours.

I've started to think of myself as a "divorcé." Nowadays, the masculine form of this adjective is never used in English.

The Bible stands between us and happiness. It's like a tree blocking the sun. Even we who don't "believe" in it — especially we — are imprisoned by its finicky strictures and all-knowing fatalism. For example, as I sit at my desk each day unable to write, I feel like Moses standing on Mount Nebo at the age of 120, forbidden to enter the Promised Land.

And why? What was Moses' sin? A mere moment of irritation, in which he struck a rock with a stick. Is that fair? Is God just? It's impossible to question the Deity. Either He doesn't exist or He's infallible; in either case we have no say.

Perhaps Moses didn't *wish* to enter the Promised Land. Perhaps his "exile" was not a punishment. Has anyone ever considered this? The Bible doesn't say that Moses regretted his expulsion.

Moses' last words were (according to Deuteronomy 33:29):

Happy art thou, O Israel: who is like unto thee, O people saved by the Lord, the shield of thy help, and who is the sword of thy excellency! and thine enemies shall be found liars unto thee; and thou shalt tread upon their high places.

A little vindictive, but not exactly depressed. Moses may have *preferred* standing on a mountain to buying a house. Maybe he liked wandering, didn't go for the settled life – like an old alcoholic hobo. Why must we always view him as cursed?

I *did* scrap that snake-in-the-house story.

Last night, in my courtyard, a tiny insect appeared to be playing a kazoo. This bug had real technique! Is there a website for virtuoso insects?

This morning my pen rolled off the desk in my "writing room," and I let it sit on the floor. A pen looks quite different far from the human hand (though close to the human foot). It was pointing toward something: perhaps Mecca (though I doubt it), perhaps the Washington Monument. A pen is like the needle of a compass – always pointing.

Women cry; men cough. Lately I've been producing strangulated coughs that seem to express a distant and anguished region of my psyche. Each time, I feel a little relief. If only I could weep!

My first language was pantomime.

Today I bought a pencil. My new plan is to write every day, for two hours, in pencil, then erase everything – rather than tearing up the paper and throwing it out. The next day I can reuse the same paper. I wonder how many times I can write and erase a single page?

Doo-wop is essentially atheist. If God really existed, why would we need teen love?

I carry an olive pit in my pocket to remind myself, in despairing moments, of the salty succulence of olives.

Perhaps I should give up writing (now that writing has given up me). But what artform should I pursue? (I still have the urge to "express myself.") Ballet? Photography? Mime?

I think I'll choose tile. When I was 12 I made a tile ashtray, and although I took no pleasure in this craft, and the ashtray was rather ugly – a mundane blue and white – I suddenly wish to try again.

The less I write, the better a writing teacher I am, I've noticed. I'm not carrying some novella in the back of my mind at all times; I can focus on my students.

Last night, in my dream, I met an illiterate woman. She was small, young – maybe 27 – with red hair. She wore three strings of pearls. I never learned her name, which seems appropriate for an illiterate person.

"You don't read at all?" I asked her. "No," she answered, smiling.

"Not a single word?" "No," she said, still smiling.

She had the innocence of the illiterate. You could see in her unlined forehead that she'd never been troubled by the written word.

What's mystifying is the death of doo-wop. The culprits are obvious: The Beatles, with three guitars and a noisy drum set. After them, voices receded, and instruments grew louder. The silence at the heart of doo-wop was lost.

After my divorce, I started to fear that I was a danger to all women. It was an illogical thought, but ineradicable. Checking out my groceries at the supermarket, I would choose a male clerk. I didn't want to injure the 16-year-old girls in mascara.

In my daily two-hour writing session, I have begun doing math problems. I began with small subtraction exercises. The first was 121 minus 96. The next was 73 minus 49.

I'm solving them faster and faster, so I'm giving myself more difficult problems. My latest one was 10,293 minus 3,742. (For some reason I prefer subtraction to addition.)

Maybe it's the novella, as a genre, that I'm tired of? William Carlos Williams once wrote: "To me all sonnets say the same thing of no importance." This may be true of the short novel. I need to invent a new fictional structure: a romance novel/philosophy essay, or science fiction/memoir.

Cynicism strikes one in three children under the age of 14.

My first memory is a meow. My family had a cat named Yellow Boy; I remember his scratchy voice. I am the only person I know whose oldest memory is auditory. Apparently, I was born to listen.

I'm either at the highest
level of obscurity or the
lowest level of fame.

There are no straight lines in nature, but there are perfect circles. Anyone who has ever dropped a stone in a pond knows this.

I've developed a new hobby: imagining which tattoo a stranger should have. I'll see a beefy man in his 40s, carrying a bag of groceries, and picture a cartoony picture of the Hope Diamond on his shoulder.

As for Joyce Carol, I think she should have a line from Montaigne – in French! – on her left forearm.

But which line? Let me consult the internet.

Here it is: "Ma vie a été remplie de terribles malheurs, dont la plupart ne se sont jamais produits." ["My life has been full of terrible misfortunes, most of which never happened."

My wife always wore her glasses while having sex. I'm not sure why – perhaps she didn't want to miss anything? It's disorienting to stick your cock in a bespectacled woman.

The concept of God always creates paradoxes. If God is universal, omnipotent, all-knowing, eternal, infinite, how can He be described? How can He be a He, for example? The first line of the Bible ("In the beginning God created the heavens and the earth") leads to unanswerable questions. How does an infinite being "create"? Is He a giant person with hands? But a giant person with hands is not infinite.

The Bible itself seems to slowly recognize this. At first God is angry and talkative, but by the end of the book, He retreats into a bleak silence.

Is it possible crows are laughing at us?

Today, during my "writing time," I drew unicorns. (I didn't even think I *liked* unicorns.) I'm a terrible artist, but it's much more fun to sketch unicorns than to write bad prose.

Joyce CO, I have noticed, never speaks about food – even the food she's eating. It's as if she disbelieves in the materiality of nourishment. (Maybe she receives her actual sustenance from books?)
Today there are Clouds of Destiny over Princeton: massive sculpted clouds untroubled by wind.

Does Joyce *like* me? Is she attracted to me? Does she pity me? Will she transform me into some minor character in her next 952-page novel?

Now I've started tearing up the pages *first* during my writing time, before I begin. On the scraps of paper, I write – then throw the pieces in the recycling bin. I find this new method liberating. If I'm going to write badly anyway, why not scribble on ripped-up paper?

The cutesT thing in

the world is baby bacteria.

My landlord planted bee balm, and large orange butterflies with black markings have been fluttering and landing on it – they look like Chinese knockoffs of Monarchs.

I woke up this morning just as a crow was giving half a caw. (I would write it as: ca.)

"The reason I became a writer is that I was very depressed as a child," Joyce Carol told me once, "and I discovered that writing changed my mood. After working on a story for 20 minutes, I was literally a different Joyce Carol than the one who had sat down."

Elderberries are ripe. What a taste! Umbrageous, sinister, woody – a 14th century taste.

Some days I feel more divorced than others – I'm not sure why. It has nothing to do with Ann, I'm sure.

Sparrow

Today I feel 70% divorced.

In my new sexual fantasy, Joyce Carol is standing over me, still in her gown, but now holding a revolver, which he points at me. "Stop jerking off and start writing!" she sternly commands, over and over.

The faces of birds are woefully incomplete. With their beady eyes and horned mouths – and non- noses – they look like hand puppets, not living creatures.

I have a new variant of my "writing" ritual. I've begun tearing up my pages smaller and smaller. Now I am a writer of confetti.

Fourteen geese flew over me, in formation (actually more of a checkmark than a V) heading south. How I envied them!

Using the dimmer switch on my ceiling light, I turned it down until it illuminated only itself.

I saw a photo of Joyce Carol in her 30s in *Harper's* magazine. One forgets how gorgeous she was. (And it was a perfectly unique beauty, self-invented.)

I often wish I had a golf cart to maneuver through Princeton. It would be the perfect vehicle for this rinky-dink town.

My marriage became an emotional knot so large and intricate that it couldn't be unraveled – so we severed it with a sword. Our last shared pleasure was slicing that knot.

This morning a crow flew down to a pear tree, plucked a yellow fruit, and took off with the pear in its mouth. It was like seeing an Aesop's fable come to life!

I went over to the tree. The pears were hard – indigestible to the human stomach.

I'm reading *Blonde*, Joyce Carol's novelized biography of Marilyn Monroe. The question of the first 80 pages is: "How does one become an icon? Is it destiny, or a series of shrewd moves?" Clearly Joyce C is asking this question about herself.

Here is a passage I chose at random [the italics are in the original:

I was afraid of them! The strong-willed ones, you had to win over fast. You didn't get a second chance. Without brothers or sisters you were alone. I was strange to them. I wanted them to like me too much, I guess. They called me Pop Eyes and Big Head, I never knew why.

"Pop Eyes" and "Big Head" could be nicknames for Joyce Carol!

Sparrow

Crows *pronounce* each word precisely.

When my first book, *Damp*, was published, I was ecstatic for four days. A brilliant light surrounded me, and by the second day the light suffused everything I touched. I remember eating a piece of toast and watching sunbeams stream out of it. My publisher was small (Polyphemus Press), but that didn't matter. I was unbendingly happy.

After the publication of my second book, the bliss lasted one day. The third book: half a day. The fourth book: no ecstasy at all.

Today was my lunch with Joyce Carol. She wore a white shirt with a lace collar and huge purple eyeglasses; she looked like an aging folksinger. "Some of us live the stories, and some of us write them," she pronounced, almost exactly in the middle of the conversation.

I seem to be doing neither, I thought.

There's a certain wistfulness in JC, as if she suspects that her last 60 books aren't as good as her first 75.

I'm thinking of buying an Etch-a-Sketch on eBay to play with during my two hours of "writing time." Is that cheating?

I gave up on *Blonde*.

Walking in the woods, I found a white pine that had fallen

over, onto the ground, but was still green. The tree flourished, though it should be dead. (In fact, the tips of the leaves showed newgrowth.)

A tree can live sideways.

I am still a writer, only a writer who produces nothing. As long as you sit at your desk every morning facing the blankness of a page you are a writer. It's only when you stop confronting that blankness that your writing career ends.

In my new masturbation fantasy, just as I'm about to ejaculate, Joyce Carol writes on my bare buttocks with a magic marker. (But I can't see what she's writing.)

Artists have struggled to paint rain for centuries, without much success. Rain is not exactly a visual phenomenon; it's a tactile one.

We speak of writers like Joyce Carol Oates as having a strong "work ethic" – but are novels actually work? Joyce Carol certainly creates many "products," but somehow "work" seems inaccurate. I would call it a "page-filling ethic."

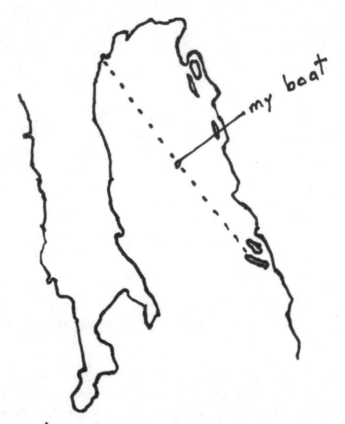

my boat

Hypoteneuse Sailor

I am sailing on
the hypotenuse
of the Adriatic.

The big question with Joyce Carol is why she had no children. Is she a narcissist – too self-interested to allow an infant into her home? Did she recognize that she had no natural talent for mothering? Was she "barren" and opposed to adoption? Are her students her children? It seems evil – brazenly intrusive – to pose these questions, but all her friends must ask them.

Today, when it was time for my daily "writing," I drove to the nearest park and sat under a pine tree. It's easier to think with branches overhead. I still didn't write anything worth preserving, but I felt happier. Why do writers always write indoors? What is so sacred about a desk?

One can be both single and divorced, the way a number can be both negative and prime.

Joyce Carol's prolificacy as a writer is connected to her personal thinness. A narrow body must produce a wide "body of work," to compensate. (And did she shun motherhood to avoid the bloatedness of pregnancy?

Doo-wop is the opposite of writing; it's an oral tradition in song. One senses that the groups didn't write down their lyrics, just committed them to memory. The vocabulary is quite limited – almost that of a child – yet the words are combined in odd ways, such as:

> Crazy little mama come knocking,
> knocking at my front door door door

(from "My Front Door" by the El Dorados). The phrase "door door door" represents the sound of knocking. The song goes on to say:

> If you got a little mama and
> you want to keep her neat
> keep your little mama off my street
> Just the term "little mama" is provocative!

I started a list of numbers I love: 1079, 2031, 1099. (They all have four digits, and zeros.)

This morning a family of sparrows are pecking on my lawn – or perhaps an ad hoc group of sparrow- strangers.

Rereading this diary, I feel that I've made Joyce Carol seem enigmatic. In fact, she is the opposite of mysterious. She is one of the most literal, direct people I've ever met. Her only mildly mysterious trait is her writing – its voluminousness and ease.

The B side of "Earth Angel" is a spectacular song called "Hey Senorita." It was originally the A side, until a perceptive DJ noticed the mournful masterpiece underneath. The title itself is absurd, and perhaps unique in world literature.

Has anyone else greeted a señorita (spelled in this version without the tilde) with slightly insulting greeting "Hey"? At that point, they continue: "Call me on the line." All in a crisp, monotonous, repetitive tone. It's one of the most unromantic love songs ever written – the opposite of its "flipside." Even the eight repetitions of "sweet mama" are pronounced rather routinely. Uptempo doo-wop songs are often quite spontaneous.

God is an onion

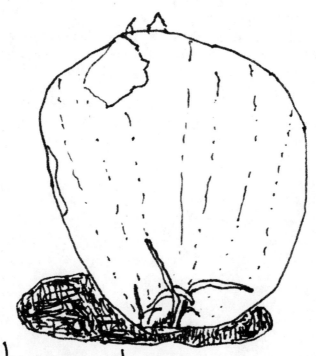

whose layers
we peel back,
weeping.

Birdsong caresses the human ear. Yes, that's the right word: "caresses."

Joyce Carol has found a way of producing multitudinous pages of prose. I have found a way of producing nothing. Which of us is superior? I kill less trees, certainly.

Lasers have made very slow progress. I imagined that by 2016 every American citizen would have one, the way women carried canisters of mace in the 1970s.

Today I wrote just four words, which I later tore up: "impressive," "clark," "maundering," "lily." ("Clark" is a medieval term for "clerk.")

Moving water always approximates speech. A stream, a brook, even water draining from a sink, make near-articulate sounds.

This morning, during my two hours, all I "wrote" was six zeros.

I always find it satisfying to watch a car make a U- turn.

Joyce Carol got a lot of publicity last week from a tweet she sent criticizing Steven Spielberg for killing mastodons. Later she revealed that this was "a kind of joke." No one expected her to perpetrate humor!

A wig is a mask

facing the sky.

Perhaps this is a clue to her vast output. Maybe her books are intended to be funny?

Today I did my two-hour writing on toilet paper. I wrote a 12 line poem about fireflies. It was a lousy poem, but looked beautiful handwritten on bright white tissue.

Doo-wop is ancient, older than the alphabet – older than words themselves. Our earliest ancestors sang songs like:

> Bom bom bom
> Dang a dang dang
> Ding a dong ding

This was before sounds were defiled by meaning. (I'm quoting the introduction to "Blue Moon" by The Marcels.)

I overheard a woman in a laundromat say: "You know how people sometimes dye toy poodles pink? Well, the best way to dye them is with Jell-O."

The town of Princeton may be preventing me from creating fiction. If I were living in a hut outside Tempe, Arizona, I suspect, my novella would be almost finished.

A bird flew into my window. It was small, perhaps a sparrow. I heard the thump, and looked up, to see the creature fly off – perhaps embarrassed?

I have a new idea: instead of trying each morning to write a novella, I will write a doo-wop song.

Rain is a symptom of a deeper problem: evaporation.

Does Joyce Carol have a secret? Does she write so intently

to remove the burden of an inner guilt? Did she kill someone as a youth – perhaps inadvertently, in a car?

Just one bird sang this morning, as I walked outside. The rest of the birds let her have a solo – which was:

    tluk tluk

            tluk

                    tluk tluk   tluk

    tluk

This morning in my bathroom: a rhombus of bright sunlight, with a nipple in one corner.

I found an *Ellery Queen Mystery Magazine* in a secondhand shop for 50 cents. It's from July 2015, and the first story, "Gun Accident: An Investigation," is by Joyce Carol. It's narrated by a 14-year-old girl named Hanna, who was asked by her seventh-grade teacher, Mrs. McClelland, to housesit. At the beginning of the story, we learn that someone was shot, but we don't know who. (This takes place in Sparta, New York, in 1961.)

I can't read Joyce Carol's books, but this short story, in a pulp magazine, called out to me. Though there are a few good sentences, the style is drab and uninventive. The virtue of the piece is the vulnerability of the narrator. She's as fragile as a ship made of willow leaves. Joyce Carol is a poet of peril. She captures the exquisite pleasure of being violated by a stranger. When the actual violence finally occurs, it's almost a relief – freeing the reader from soul-eating anxiety.

Sometimes crows make sounds like car horns. It's not that they're exactly *imitating* noises they hear; rather they have influences, like jazz musicians.

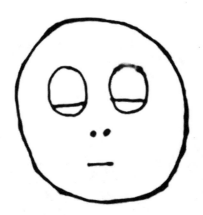

Emoticons have replaced irony.

Sparrow

Here is my doo-wop song:

       ooeeoeeiiiiiyiii
       No harm
       No harm
       No harm

       I will do you
       No harm
       No harm
       No harm

       If you do me
       No harm
       No harm
       No harm

       My darling, I adore you;
       You walk in my rain.
       My darling, I adore you;
       You swallow my shame.

       I will do you
       No harm
       No harm
       No harm

If you do me
No harm
No harm
No harm

My darling, never leave me;
I need you like bread.
My darling, never leave me;
I am in your debt.

I will do you
No harm
No harm
No harm

If you do me
No harm
No harm
No harm

[The beginning is a falsetto solo. I can hear it in my mind, but it's difficult to notate in letters.]

Joyce Carol's fascination with Twitter – she has produced, so far, approximately 31,200 tweets – is both surprising and logical.

Certain raindrops are more adherent than others. Today a very light rain fell, clinging to everything.

The existence of cameras suggests that something somewhere is beautiful.

This is the best job I will ever have; I will never work in the Ivy League again. It was a miracle that I even received this appointment. The rumor is that an important novelist canceled at the last minute, so they called me. This assignment is the apex of my career; starting this fall my arc will slowly descend. (Or maybe not so slowly.)

Is that why I can't write? I thought I wrote to express my inner self; maybe I was just advancing my career. Now that my future is doomed, why produce a new book?

I saw six crows standing at the base of a tree, under a cloudy sky. They looked like mourners at a small Victorian funeral.

For some reason, veggie burgers are never made with potatoes. Why is this?

Joyce Carol's writing isn't exactly writing – it's more like speaking. Her 135 books (and counting) are one vast monologue delivered to the silent American people.

Luckily, marriage isn't permanent. You can escape anytime you want, back into the treacherous pleasures of solitude.

This morning: a hard rain. Afterwards I went out and saw a long leaf of grass beaten down to the ground. Atop the leaf was a row of raindrops, arranged just like words in a sentence. In this manner does nature "write."

"Sh'boom" by The Chords asserts:

> Life could be a dream,
> sweetheart!

It is, I suspect, a deeply political song. "Sh'boom" raises the question: why can't we perfect this world? The year was 1954 – the very beginning of the Civil Rights movement.

> Oh, life could be a dream,
> Sh'boom

If only all my precious plans would come true…

"Sh'boom" reached #9, but was covered by The Crew-

Cuts (who were, as their name suggests, white) then held #1 for nine weeks.

Joyce Carol gave a reading at Langley Hall. It's a yearly tradition. I was surprised how poorly it was attended – mostly teenagers and septuagenarians. The old folks were her friends and colleagues; the youth had been assigned to the event by their professors. The esteemed author read a short story that had recently appeared in *The Suwanee Review*. She spoke hurriedly, stumbling over a number of words. She seemed slightly embarrassed to be Joyce Carol Oates.

Joyce Carol is an intimate person, I suspect. She is slightly suffocated by crowds. Her favorite activities are writing manuscripts and tweeting.

I wish one could hire a wife for an evening, to attend a dinner party, receive a short, affectionate massage, and break the monotony of bachelorhood.

How nice to be *occasionally* married!

Certain crows stutter: "C-c-c-c-c-cuh-c-c-cuh."

I have met four or five other novelists in my life. All of them were soft-spoken, unpopular people – almost like walking novellas.

Here is a tweet of Joyce Carol's from January 31:

> Query for evolutionary biologists: are human
> beings the only species that have "baby teeth"? –
> & what is the purpose of "baby teeth"?

It's grammatically incorrect!

I ordered the lentil pizza at Baroff 's. It's a pizza topped with a lentil stew, including spinach and cauliflower. It tastes like two peasants from two nations, each carrying dinner, collided.

When I was a teenager I would half-steal books. I'd go to a bookstore, make sure the clerk couldn't see, hide a novel under my shirt, and walk outside. I'd read a few pages, then return the book. No one ever suspected.

The human voice is the most fluid of all instruments. Doo-wop has that silky, swooping agility only song can achieve.

Our species has lost the ability to live outdoors. We're like colonists on Mars who must dwell within bubbles of atmosphere. Only a few thousand tribal people, and a few dozen hobos, live in the wild.

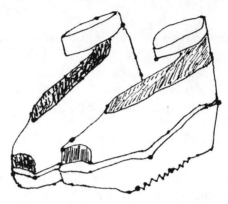

The opposite of sensible shoes are senseless shoes.

Crows don't migrate. They like it just fine where they are.

A balloon is a way of preserving air. If your mother is dying, you might tell her to blow up a balloon, so you'll have that remnant of her – like a saint's relic – for months. Likewise, one might save a celebrity's breath in a balloon to exhibit to friends: "Believe it or not, this is Tom Cruise's carbon dioxide!"

Should I ask Joyce Carol to blow up a balloon for me?

Each morning all the birds introduce themselves, like English gentry at a dinner party.

I cut two small triangles in my underwear, with a scissors.

They are small triangles, about ½ inch on a side. I did it for no reason, unless aesthetics is a reason.

Doo-wop may be the most organic music; the four singers function together like organs of the body: heart, lungs, intestines, brain.

We speak of two people "finding" love, but never of them "losing" love, though love may be lost – the way one loses the lease to an apartment.

Another of Joyce Carol's tweets:

> Robot cops could be programmed not to react to someone's skin color. Wouldn't that be preferable to present-day cops?

They're better-written than her novels!

You know how you sometimes walk into a Dollar Store planning to buy AA batteries and leave 20 minutes later with two large aluminum pans for frying chicken? You completely forgot the batteries, and can't remember why you bought the pans? My marriage was like that.

I am losing my faith in fiction. What exactly is the point of creating imaginary stories? To give the reader an emotional experience? And how enduring is that experience? After reading my book, the reader just moves on to another book. And after that, another book. What difference does it make if my book exists or not? Let people just read the book before mine and the book after mine and leave mine out.

One of my colleagues saw Joyce Carol in the parking lot of Whole Foods. Clearly the noted author had forgotten where her car was: she wandered around helplessly.

There are two paths to wisdom: the path of happiness and the path of sorrow. For many, marriage is the path of happiness. You have a person to love, who loves you in return. Together you raise children, who love you even more – and eventually, grandchildren, who love you unceasingly. You learn to give, to receive, to negotiate. Divorce, on the other hand, is the path of sadness. You are isolated, solitary, forgotten. You learn the heroism of silence.

The Lonely Woman With the Dog and the soft- voiced boyfriend are still together! I saw them walking into her apartment carrying groceries, chatting nimbly. They still radiate unhurried delight.

Rock 'n roll is impulsive; doo-wop is studied. It's one art-form where you *hear* the hours of practice.

The way The Lonely Woman With the Dog and her boyfriend stand together, I can tell they met over the Internet.

All money is made from rocks and trees. Coins are melted-down rocks; paper currency is pulped trees.

Joyce Carol has almost the exact personality of an eight year old. Someone as childlike as her could only survive in a university.

How about a detective novel starring Joyce Carol Oates? A young student dies at Princeton: a female poet. Detectives are stumped. They interview Joyce Carol, because she knew the victim. The famous writer becomes fascinated with the mystery, dusts off her magnifying glass, and begins searching for clues...

Living alone is like singing a cappella. One can achieve a certain purity of tone that is impossible with "accompaniment."
A worker is expected to produce. A bricklayer must lay bricks. A writer must lay down sentences. I'm not doing my job; I should be fired.

Doo-wop is almost anonymous. Unlike Frank Sinatra or Bing Crosby, the individual singers are unknown – sometimes they haven't even been photographed. Doo-wop musicians perform under a collective name like The Cleftones, obscure as Franciscan monks.

Joyce Carol's productivity is freakish. Books poor out of her like cupcakes from a bakery. Her fecundity is almost obscene. Yet Joyce Carol makes graphomania appear natural and normal. Compared to her, all other writers are repressed, inhibited.

I wish I never had to eat out of plastic. If only you could buy yogurt in earthenware pots!

Doo-wop is best heard on vinyl records. A CD, or even a cassette, doesn't capture the echoing overtones. As I move from place to place, I carry my 82 doo-wop records.

I wonder what Joyce Carol thinks of doo-wop?
As the summer ends, I begin to think about death – including my own personal death. This body I walk around in has a limited warranty. Eventually it will develop a dysfunction that contemporary medicine can't fix. My writing has already died, to prepare me for oblivion.

Crows sometimes sing in triplets:
        ca-ca-ca, ca-ca-ca, ca-ca-ca

just like doo-wop singers.

My latest theory about Joyce Carol: she writes to scare herself. Almost all her stories have a whiff of unspeakable evil. In her tedious daily life, devoid of real danger, Joyce Carol craves terror.

Trees resemble their mothers and fathers, just as we do.

My personal speechlessness – my inability to write – is a tribute to Joyce Carol.

Divorce surprised me. I never expected that my marriage would fail – I guess because my parents never split up. I had forgotten that divorce existed.

But I recommend it to anyone. It's like being reborn; much more than marriage is. Right now I feel like I'm 11 years old. If I wrote self-help books, my next one would be *The Joy of Divorce*.

Bad news for Joyce Carol-on-Twitter fans: she's begun re-tweeting! Much of her feed now is lamentable news from PETA, and other animal- loving websites. This is the fourth stage of her tweets that I've noticed. The stages are:

1) Sentences so long they were divided into two or three tweets.

2) Long statements just under 140 characters.

3) Photographs (often of her cats).

4) Incessant retweeting.

Has Joyce Carol run out of public thoughts?

My new book is an attack on the literary establishment for ignoring my last 4 books.

The Lonely Woman with the Dog has quietly moved out of her apartment. I saw the smiling boyfriend helping her carry boxes. He is so selfless around her!

What do you call someone who sits at a desk two hours a day producing nothing? "Writer" is definitely the wrong word. Maybe "sitter"? "Daydreamer"? "Lazybones"? "Fool"?

The Princeton Diary

Each time I meet with Joyce Carol, she is livelier and more curious. Perhaps it's the nature of friendship – or is she aware that I have written nothing for eight months? (Of course, I haven't told her, but maybe she can sense it.) Is she *studying* me as an example of "speechlessness"?

I went walking on a horse path in Glendover. Am I the only person who finds horse droppings beautiful?

Now in my masturbation fantasy, Joyce Carol no longer speaks; she just coughs spasmodically.

A crow will often perch at the very top of a tree, as if trees were created as pedestals.

Joyce Carol was wise never to have children, because a mother sees the world philosophically, and JC does not. The way she writes about teenage girls, you know she never had to drive one to dance class.

Real connoisseurs of doo-wop study the music geographically. Some aficionados prefer Baltimorean doo-wop; some champion the Detroit style. At the moment I'm interested in New Jersey singers, especially The Royal Teens.

The Royal Teens were unusual – almost unique – in that they played their own instruments. Johnny Trenton, the sax player, was a gifted musician. At the age of 17, he played the inventive solos on "Who Wears Short Shorts?" (plus, he cowrote the song). This novelty number, the Royal Teens' first and greatest hit, is the missing link between doo-wop and jazz.

I once had a vivid dream in which I met Pablo Picasso. "Do you know why we are famous?" he asked, sitting across the table from me. By "we" he clearly meant all renowned people. "It's because of our *names*."

Within the dream, everything suddenly became clear. The name "Pablo Picasso" could only belong to a historic person. This is true also of my fellow Princeton professor. "Joyce Carol Oates" is a perfect name. The first word suggests James Joyce; the second is a type of song associated with Christmas; the surname is one of the basic grains. The three- part name seems to say: "James Joyce is caroling among the oats" – a visionary image.

And the sound of each word is perfect. "Joyce Carol Wheat" is a horrible name, as is "Joyce Carol Rice."

In fact, Joyce Carol adores James Joyce. She considers *Ulysses* the greatest novel in the English language and called it: "an opera-like work that is best appreciated if read and reread, aloud if possible, with an awareness of the 'jocoseriousness' that underlies each passage."

And "Joyce Carol Oates" is a jocoserious name.